12.99   11/17/11   3148470

W9-CDN-540

KILLER KOALAS

KOALAS

FROM OUTER SPACE

and Lots of Other Very Bad Stuff
that Will Make Your Brain Explode!

A FEIWEL AND FRIENDS BOOK
An Imprint of Macmillan

KILLER KOALAS FROM OUTER SPACE. Text copyright © 2004, 2010 by Backyard Stories Pty Ltd. Illustrations copyright © 2010 by Terry Denton. All rights reserved. Printed in September 2011 in the United States of America by R. R. Donnelley & Sons Company, Crawfordsville, Indiana. For information, address Feiwel and Friends, 175 Fifth Avenue, New York, N.Y. 10010.

Library of Congress Cataloging-in-Publication Data Available
ISBN: 978-0-312-36789-3

Book design by Elizabeth Tardiff
Portions of this book were originally published in Australia
as The Bad Book and The Very Bad Book

Feiwel and Friends logo designed by Filomena Tuosto

First Edition: 2011

10 9 8 7 6 5 4 3 2 1
mackids.com

KILLER KOALAS FROM OUTER SPACE

and Lots of Other Very Bad Stuff that Will Make Your Brain Explode!

by
Andy Griffiths

illustrations by
Terry Denton

Killer Koalas from Outer Space

Killer koalas from outer space:
They look cute and cuddly,
but they'll rip off your face!

They come here disguised
as cute marsupials,
but they're really face-ripping
extraterrestrials!

So, if I were you, from this place I would race
before those koalas (with unseemly haste)
get out their claws and
RIP OFF YOUR FACE!

THE END

Very Bad Mary, Quite Contrary

Very Bad Mary, quite contrary,
how does your garden grow?
With poison ivy, prickles, and thistles,
and spiky weeds all in a row?

Little Willy

Eating more than he was able,
Willy died at the breakfast table.
"Please, Mama," said little Meg.
"May I have his other egg?"

Bad Mommy and Daddy and the Volcano

THE END

The Old Woman
Who Lived in a Poo

There was an old woman
who lived in a poo.

She had so many flies,
she didn't know what to do!

She gave them some broth
and put them to bed.

Then sprayed them
with fly spray
until they were dead.

The Very Bad Ant and the Big Red Shiny Space Rocket

Once upon a time, there was an ant. It *looked* like an ordinary ant, but it wasn't. It was a very bad ant.

And the very bad ant went along the ground and came to a stick.
And the very bad ant went up the stick. And the very bad ant went over the stick.
And the very bad ant went down the stick.

And the very bad ant went along the ground
and came to a blade of grass.
And the very bad ant went up the blade of grass.
And the very bad ant went over the blade of grass.
And the very bad ant went down the blade of grass.

And then it stopped.

And then it started again.

And the very bad ant went along the ground
and came to a big red shiny space rocket.
And the very bad ant went up
the big red shiny space rocket.
And the very bad ant
went *into* the big red shiny space rocket.

And the very bad ant pressed the START button!

WHOOSH! went the big red shiny space rocket as it blasted off into space.

"COME BACK WITH OUR BIG RED SHINY SPACE ROCKET!" shouted the astronauts. But it was no use. The very bad ant couldn't hear them above the roar of the rocket, and even if it could have, it would have kept on flying anyway because, as I think I have already mentioned, it was a *very bad* ant.

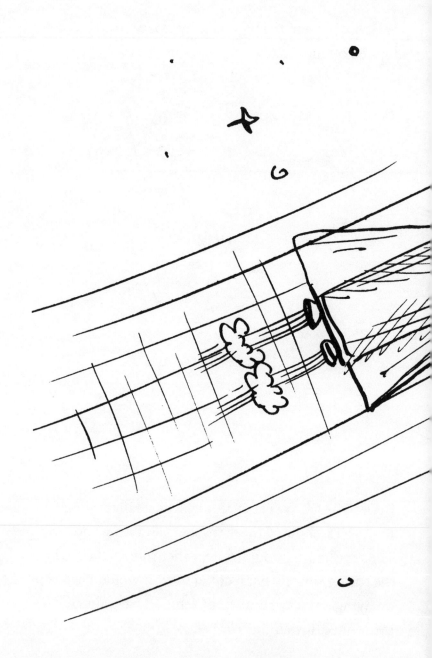

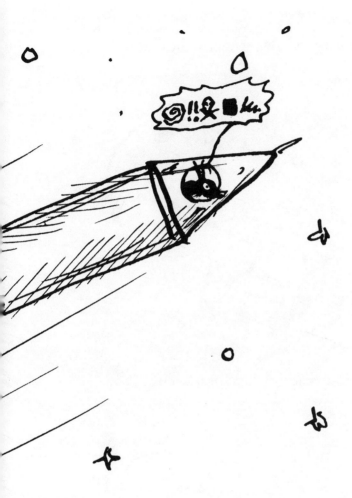

19

And the very bad ant went past the moon.

And the very bad ant went past Venus.

And the very bad ant went past Mercury and headed straight toward the sun, which was a very dangerous thing to do because the sun is very, very hot. Especially when you get really close to it.

But do you think the very bad ant cared?
No, of course not.
It didn't even have its seat belt fastened
or its space helmet on!

The very bad ant just flew the big red shiny space
rocket straight into the sun and was burned to death.
Which wasn't very nice. But not very surprising,
because it was a bad ant. A *very* bad ant.

THE END

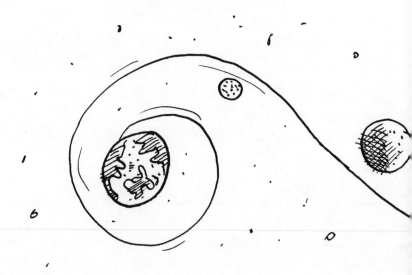

Very Bad Koala Riddles

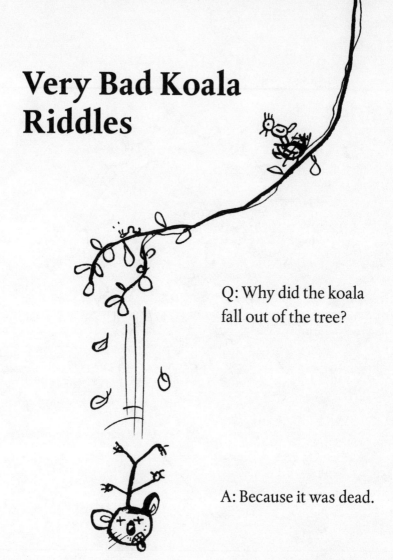

Q: Why did the koala fall out of the tree?

A: Because it was dead.

Q: Why did
the second koala
fall out of the tree?

A: It was hit
by the first koala.

Q: Why did
the third koala
fall out of the tree?

Weeee!

A: It thought it was a game,
and joined in.

25

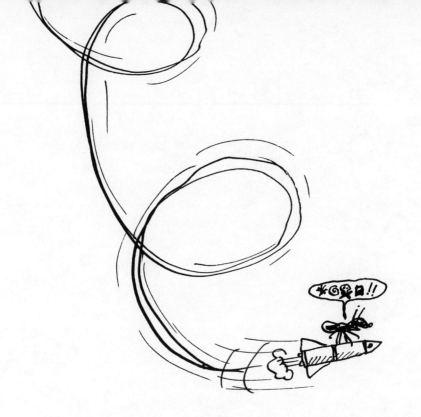

Brian and His Very Bad Idea

THE END

The Three Bad Guys
and the Very Bad Idea

Once upon a time, there were three bad guys:
a big bad guy, a medium-sized bad guy, and
a little bad guy.

One day, the three bad guys were sitting around in
their clubhouse thinking up bad stuff to do when
the big bad guy said, "Hey, I've got a very bad idea!
Let's not wash our hands after going to the toilet!"

"That *is* a very bad idea!" said the medium-sized bad guy, "and let's *also* not wash them after picking our noses!"

"Yeah!" said the little bad guy. "And let's *especially* not wash them after touching pets and other animals!"

And the three bad guys all high-fived each other and agreed that not washing their hands was a *very bad idea* and they began not washing their hands immediately.

31

As it turned out, the three bad guys were right; not washing their hands *was* a very bad idea because it wasn't long before their hands were covered in really nasty germs that crawled up their arms, invaded their bodies, and caused sniffles, rashes, fevers, coughing, vomiting, diarrhoea, hepatitis A, hepatitis B, halitosis, tuberculosis, myxomatosis, supercalifragilisticexpialidosis, and tummyache . . . all of which made the three bad guys feel *very* bad indeed!

THE END

Very Rude Animals

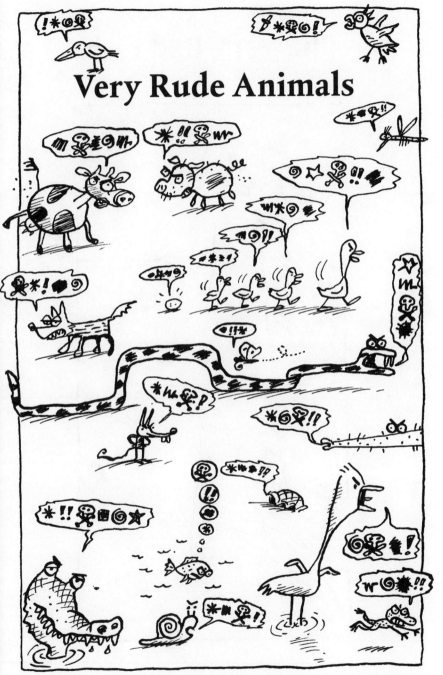

The Very Bad Fish

THE END

37

The Dog that Fell Apart

Once upon a time, there was a dog.

One day, the dog's tail fell off.

The next day, his legs fell off.

The next day, his nose fell off.

The next day, his ears fell off.

The next day, his head fell off.

The next day was Tuesday.

THE END

40

THE END

41

Very Bad Farmer Riddles

Q: What did the farmer say when he couldn't
find his tractor?

A: "Where's my tractor?"

Q: What did the farmer say
when he found his tractor?

A: "There's my tractor!"

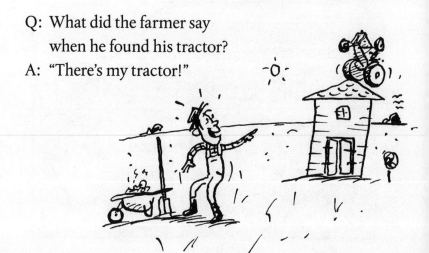

Q: What do you call a farmer with
   a tractor on his head?
A: Dead.

Very Bad Invention No. 1:
The Non-flush Toilet

Very Bad Invention No. 2: Non-elastic Underpants

Nobody Likes Me

Nobody likes me, everybody hates me,
think I'm gonna eat some worms.
First you chop their heads off,
then you squeeze their guts out.
Ooh, what a horrible mess . . . YUCK!

Bad Macdonald

Bad Macdonald had a really stinky farm,
ee-i-ee-i *pee-uw!*
And on that farm, he had a dead pig
with its guts coming out,
ee-i-ee-i *pee-uw!*
With pig guts here,
and pig guts there.
Here some guts!
There some guts!
Everywhere, some pig guts!
Bad Macdonald had a really stinky farm,
ee-i-ee-i *pee-uw!*

Bad Macdonald had a really stinky farm,
ee-i-ee-i *pee-uw!*
And on that farm, he had a dead cow
with its guts coming out,
ee-i-ee-i *pee-uw!*
With cow guts here,
and cow guts there.
Here some guts!
There some guts!
Everywhere, some cow guts!
Bad Macdonald had a really stinky farm,
ee-i-ee-i *pee-uw!*

cow brain
juice.

Lizard.

Bad Macdonald had a really stinky farm,
ee-i-ee-i *pee-uw!*
And on that farm, he had a dead horse
with its guts coming out,
ee-i-ee-i *pee-uw!*
With horse guts here,
and horse guts there.
Here some guts!
There some guts!
Everywhere, some horse guts!
Bad Macdonald had a really stinky farm,
ee-i-ee-i *pee-uw!*

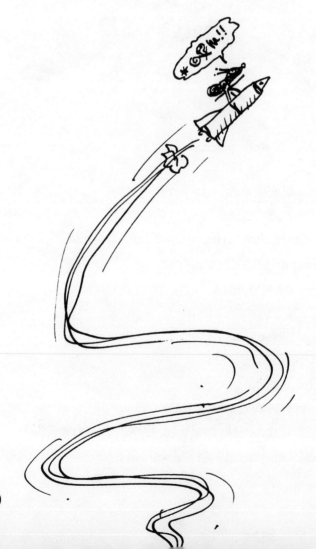

The Boy Who Ate Dead Flies

ONE DAY, A LITTLE BOY WAS SITTING BY A WINDOW WHEN HE FOUND A DEAD FLY.

Mom, can I eat this dead fly?

Don't be silly, dear, that's disgusting! You'll make yourself sick.

BUT THE BOY DIDN'T LISTEN TO HIS MOTHER.

I'm going to do it anyway.

FIRST, HE ATE THE WINGS.

THEN, HE ATE THE EYES.

THEN, HE ATE THE BODY.

THE BOY WAITED FOR A LITTLE WHILE, BUT HE DIDN'T FEEL SICK AT ALL.

SO, THE BOY ATE ANOTHER DEAD FLY.

AND ANOTHER . . .

AND ANOTHER . . .

AND ANOTHER . . .

SUDDENLY, HE BEGAN TO FEEL STRANGE.

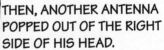

Urk! I feel strange!

THEN, WITHOUT WARNING, AN ANTENNA POPPED OUT OF THE LEFT SIDE OF HIS HEAD.

THEN, ANOTHER ANTENNA POPPED OUT OF THE RIGHT SIDE OF HIS HEAD.

54

THE END

55

Very Stupid Riddles

Q: Why couldn't the cat drink its milk?
A: Because it didn't have a face.

Q: What's red and not there?
A: No tomato.

Q: What's brown and looks out the window?
A: A poo on stilts.

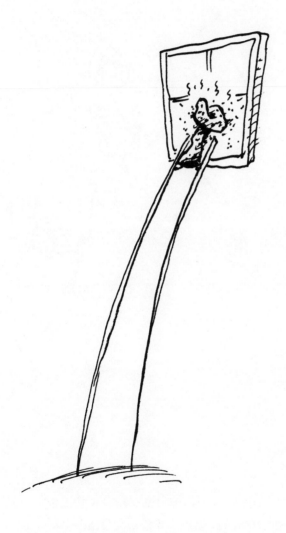

Very Bad Penguin Joke

Two penguins were standing on an iceberg.
One turned to the other and said, "Radio."

The Very Bad Road

61

65

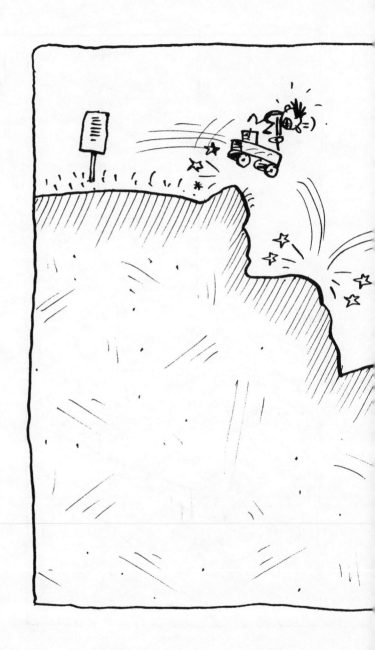

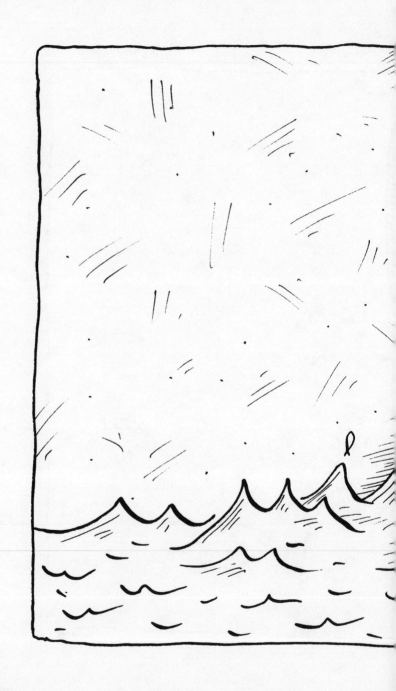

THE END

The Sad Bad Bad-man

Once upon a time,
 there was a sad bad bad-man.
The sad bad bad-man was sad
 because he was bad
 at being bad.

So, the sad bad bad-man
went to sad bad bad-man's school

where they taught
sad bad bad-men
how to be good at being
good bad-men,
instead of being good at being
sad bad bad-men.

And the sad bad bad-man stopped being sad
    and became glad
because he learned how to be a good bad-man
    who was good at being bad,
    instead of bad at being bad.

In fact,

the ex-sad bad bad-man

was so good at being bad

that he became

the gladdest ex-sad bad bad-man

in the history of

sad bad bad-men

who stopped being sad bad bad-men

and became

glad good bad-men.

THE END

Mud Brown
and the Seven Slobs

Once upon a slime, there was a disgusting princess called Mud Brown. She lived in a stinking bog with seven slobs called Stinky, Filthy, Snotty, Messy, Grubby, Sloppy, and Robert.

Mud Brown and the seven slobs ate dirt, put mud in their underpants, sneezed in each other's faces, shoved handfuls of worms in their ears, and never EVER brushed their teeth.

One day, an unhandsome prince called Prince
Poopy-pants came riding through the forest on a filthy
warthog and saw Mud Brown and the seven slobs
having a wild mud fight.

Prince Poopy-pants looked at Mud Brown's filthy
clothes, dirty face, matted hair, and ears full of nasty
wriggling worms, and fell in love with her at once.

He leapt from his warthog and waded into the bog toward her. "You are the dirtiest, most perfectly despicable princess I have ever laid my beady, bloodshot eyes on!" he said. "Will you marry me?"

Mud Brown scooped up a big handful of mud and slammed it right in the prince's face. "Of course I will," she said. "I've been waiting all my life for someone as unhandsome, unappealing, and unhygienic as you!"

Prince Poopy-pants and Mud Brown embraced and kissed but, unfortunately, as neither of them had ever cleaned their teeth in their entire lives, the combined stench of their terrible breath formed a cloud so toxic that it not only killed them both, but also Stinky, Filthy, Snotty, Messy, Grubby, Sloppy, and Robert. And nobody lived ever after.

THE END

Mommy, Mommy!

Son: Mommy, Mommy! What's a
    werewolf?
Mom: Shut up and comb your face!

Son: Mommy, Mommy! Are we really
    vampires?
Mom: Shut up and drink your soup
    before it clots!

Son: Mommy, Mommy! I'm scared of
    zombies!
Mom: Shut up and eat your brains while
    they're still warm!

THE END

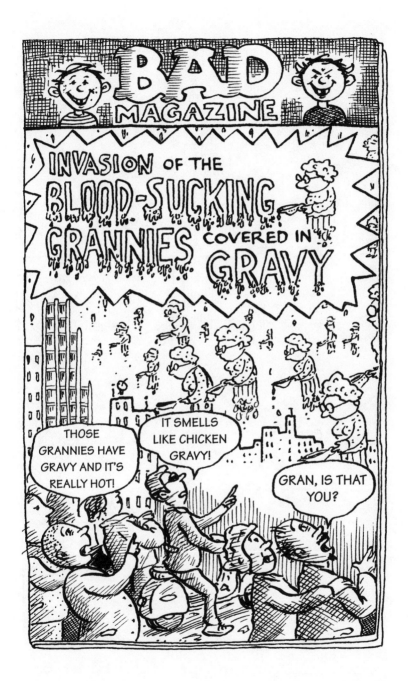

83

85

The Very Bad Giraffe

THE END

The Very Bad Dentist

THE END

Very Bad Tree Riddles

Q: Why did the man
cut down the tree?

A: Because it was there.

Q: Why didn't the man
cut down the tree?

A: Because it
wasn't there.

Q: Why did the tree
cut down the man?

A: Because
it was a bad tree.

Brian and His Very, Very Bad Idea

THE END

The Girl Who Slammed Doors

There once was a girl who slammed doors
from morning to night without pause.
　　She slammed them so hard
　　that the rooms fell apart,
and all that was left were the floors.

Very Bad Hippo Joke

Two hippos are in a swamp
with water up to their eyes.
One looks at the other and says,
"I don't know why, but I keep thinking
it's Tuesday."

The Boy Who Forgot His Head Because It Wasn't Screwed On

Once upon a time, there was a very forgetful boy. He would forget to do his chores. He would forget to do his homework. And sometimes, he would even forget to put his pants on before he went to school!

You forgot your pants!

"Honestly!" his mother would say, shaking her head. "You'd forget your head if it wasn't screwed on!"

One day, the boy said to himself,
"I wonder if my head really *is* screwed on?"
The boy put his hands over his ears
and twisted his head to the right.
It moved a little.

He gave another twist.
It moved a little more.

He gave it one more twist and,
to his surprise, his head came
completely off his body.

"Cool!" said the boy. "My head really does screw on . . . and off!" And he screwed it on.

And off.

And on.

And off.

And on.

And off.

He was about to screw it on again when he heard his best friend calling from outside and he ran off to play, completely forgetting to screw his head back on, just as his mother had predicted.

The boy's head sat
on the table in front
of the window where the
boy had left it. Pretty
soon, however, the wind
started to blow and . . .

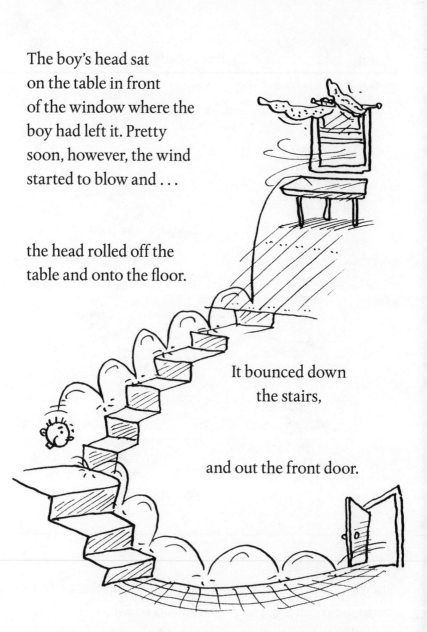

the head rolled off the
table and onto the floor.

It bounced down
the stairs,

and out the front door.

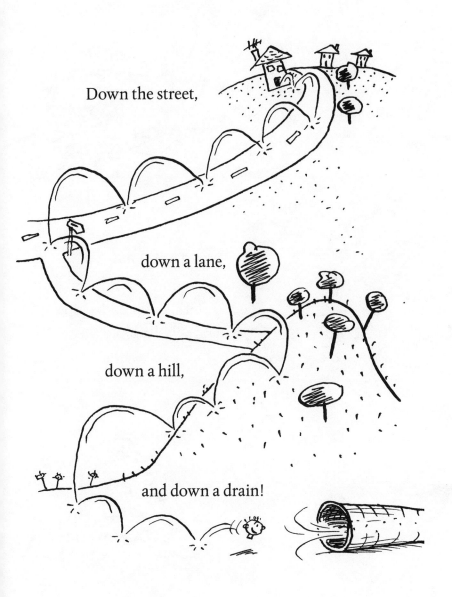

Down the street,

down a lane,

down a hill,

and down a drain!

Along a dark
and slimy pipe,
past frogs and toads
and rats that bite!

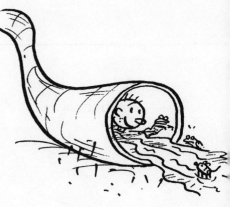

The head rolled on
until, eventually,
it slid out of the pipe
and splashed into the sea ...

where it was swallowed
by a fish ...

which was swallowed
by a *very* big fish . . .

which was swallowed
by a very, *very* big fish . . .

which was swallowed by
a very, very, very *small* fish . . .

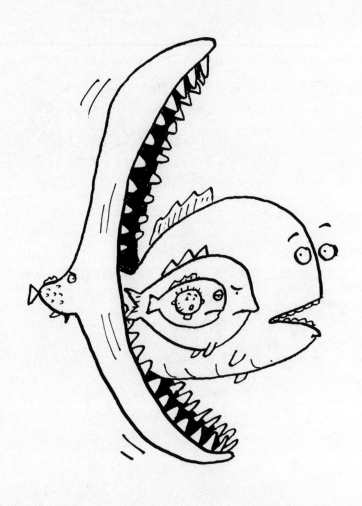

with a very, very, very *big* mouth!

And

the

very,

very, very

small fish

with the

very,

very,

very

big mouth

was caught by

a fisherman,

who took it home,
cut it open,
and out rolled
the boy's head!

So, the fisherman did what he did with all
the interesting things he found inside the fish
he caught: He put it on eBay and, after a
furious bidding war, it was bought by a
little old lady who cleaned it, polished it up,
and used it as a bowling ball.

STRIKE!

As for the boy,
don't feel too sorry for him.
He soon forgot he'd ever had
a head and lived happily—
and headlessly—
ever after.

THE END

Tarzan the Monkey Man

Tarzan the monkey man,
swinging on a rubber band.
Along came Superman
and kicked him in the garbage can!

The Adventures of the Dog Poo Family

PART 1

THE END

The Adventures of the Dog Poo Family

PART 2

THE END

The Adventures of the Dog Poo Family

PART 3

THE END

The Very Bad Holiday

DAY 1: STEP IN DOG POO

DAY 2: SWIMMING POOL
EMPTY

DAY 3: SWIMMING POOL
FULL OF DOG POO

DAY 4: CHASED BY LIONS

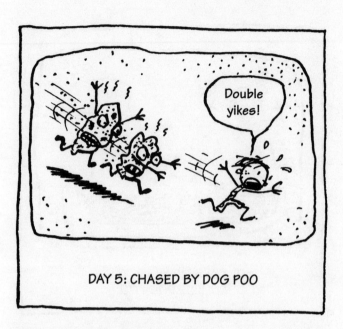

DAY 5: CHASED BY DOG POO

DAY 6: ICE CREAM FALLS
OFF STICK

THE END

The Very Bad Guide to Good and Bad

Cute fluffy kittens
BAD!

Zombie kittens
GOOD!

Cute fluffy koalas
BAD!

Killer koalas who rip off your face
GOOD!

Helping old people cross the road
BAD!

Helping old people rob banks
GOOD!

Giving people presents
BAD!

Cough!
Cough!

Giving people germs
GOOD!

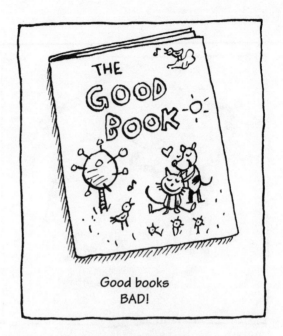

Good books
BAD!

Bad books
GOOD!

Little Bad Riding Hood

Once upon a time, there was a bad little
girl called Little Bad Riding Hood.

One day,
her mother said to her,
"Little Bad Riding Hood,
your grandmother is
very sick.

Would you
do me a favor
and take her
this basket of food,
drink,
and vital medicine
without which,
she will surely die?"

And Little Bad Riding Hood said,

"No."

THE END

Peter, Peter,
Junk food Eater

Peter, Peter, junk food eater
guzzled lemonade by the liter.
gobbled jelly beans by the ton
ate ice cream cakes and sticky buns.

He began to grow and swell
and was not looking very well.
He drank a milk shake to quench his thirst.
He groaned,
   and burped,
     and then
    he burst.

Bad Daddy and the Pencil Sharpener

137

THE END

Very Bad
Knock-knock Jokes

Knock knock!
Who's there?
Poo-poo.
Poo-poo who?
Poo-poo wee-wee.

Knock knock!
Who's there?
Poo-poo wee-wee.
Poo-poo wee-wee who?
Poo-poo wee-wee poo-poo wee-wee.

Knock knock!
Who's there?
Alice.
Alice who?
Alice Poo-poo wee-wee poo-poo wee-wee.

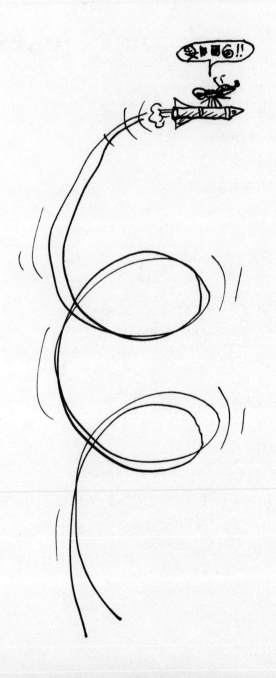

Brian and His Very, Very Very Bad Idea

THE END

The Very Bad Builder

Once upon a time,
there was a very bad builder.

Everybody would say to him,
"Can you fix it?"
and he would say,
"No,
I can't."

THE END

Badword Puzzle

CLUES

Across

1. Not good (3)
2. Wicked (3)
3. Naughty (3)
5. DAB backwards (3)
6. Shoddy (3)
8. Faulty (3)
9. Imperfect (3)
10. Terrible (3)
11. Off or sour (3)
13. Disobedient (3)
14. Harmful (3)
16. Rotten (3)
17. Putrid (3)
18. Good-for-nothing (3)

Down

1. Evil (3)
3. Rhymes with sad (3)
4. Dreadful (3)
5. Rude (3)
6. Nasty (3)
7. Gross (3)
8. Offensive (3)
10. Misbehaved (3)
11. Useless (3)
12. Worthless (3)
13. Vile (3)
14. Atrocious (3)
15. Sinful (3)
16. Abominable (3)
17. Despicable (3)

Solution:

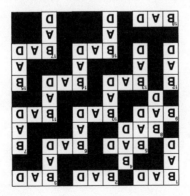

147

The Very Bad Story

Once upon a time, things were bad. Then, things got very bad. And just when everybody thought things couldn't possibly get any badder, they did.

They got very, very bad.

THE END

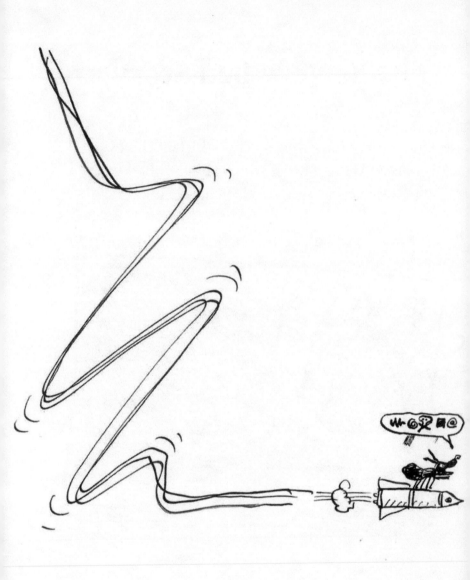

The Very, Very Bad Story

Once upon a time, things were very, very bad. And just when everybody thought things couldn't possibly get any badder, they did. They got twice as bad.

Then they got three times as bad.

Then they got four thousand, eight hundred, and seventy-three and five-sixteenths badder still.

THE END

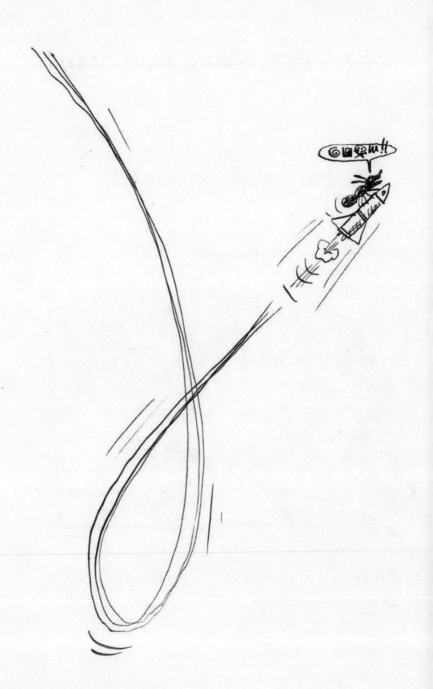

The Very, Very, Very Bad Story

Once upon a time, things were four thousand, eight hundred, and seventy-three and five-sixteenths badder than the time things were three times as bad as the time things were twice as bad as the time when they were just very, very bad.

In fact, things were SO bad that it made all the previous bad days seem like the good old days, and the memory of those good old bad days made everybody cry and feel very sorry for themselves and feel even badder than they already did.

But eventually, people started saying, "Hey, we can't just sit around crying all day and feeling bad. We should try to fix things and make everything good again."

So everybody got up, wiped their tears away, stopped feeling sorry for themselves, and tried to make things good again.

But it was no use. The more they tried to make things good again, the badder things got. Things just got badder and

badder and badder and

badder and badder and badder and badder and badder
and badder and badder and badder and badder and
badder and badder and badder and badder and badder
and badder and badder and badder and badder and
badder and badder and badder and badder and badder
and badder and badder and badder and badder and
badder and badder and badder and badder and badder
and badder and badder and badder and badder and
badder and badder and badder and badder and badder
and badder and badder and badder and badder and
badder and badder and badder and badder and badder
and badder and badder and badder and badder and
badder and badder and badder and badder and badder
and badder and badder and badder and badder and
badder and badder and badder and badder and badder
and badder and badder and badder and badder and
badder and badder and badder and badder and badder
and badder and badder and badder and badder and
badder and badder and badder and badder and badder
and badder and badder and badder and badder and
badder and badder and badder and badder and badder
and badder and badder and badder and badder and
badder and badder and badder and badder and badder
and badder and badder and badder and badder and

badder and badder and badder and badder and badder
and badder and badder and badder and badder and
badder and badder and badder and badder and badder
and badder and badder and badder and badder and
badder and badder and badder and badder and badder
and badder and badder and badder and badder and
badder and badder and badder and badder and badder
and badder and badder and badder and badder and
badder and badder and badder and badder and badder
and badder and badder and badder and badder and
badder and badder and badder and badder and badder
and badder and badder and badder and badder and
badder and badder and badder and badder and badder
and badder and badder and badder and badder and
badder and badder and badder and badder and badder
and badder and badder and badder and badder and
badder and badder and badder and badder and badder
and badder and badder and badder and badder and
badder and badder and badder and badder and badder
and badder and badder and badder and badder and
badder and badder and badder and badder and badder
and badder and badder and badder and badder and
badder and badder and badder and badder and badder
and badder and badder and badder and badder and

badder and badder and badder and badder and badder
and badder and badder and badder and badder and
badder and badder and badder and badder and badder
and badder and badder and badder and badder and
badder and badder and badder and badder and badder
and badder and badder and badder and badder and
badder and badder and badder and badder and badder
and badder and badder and badder and badder and
badder and badder and badder and badder and badder
and badder and badder and badder and badder and
badder and badder and badder and badder and badder
and badder and badder and badder and badder and
badder and badder and badder and badder and badder
and badder and badder and badder and badder and
badder and badder and badder and badder and badder
and badder and badder and badder and badder and
badder and badder and badder and badder and badder
and badder and badder and badder and badder and
badder and badder and badder and badder and badder
and badder and badder and badder and badder and
badder and badder and badder and badder and badder
and badder and badder and badder and badder and
badder and badder and badder and badder and badder
and badder and badder and badder and badder and

badder and badder and badder and badder and badder
and badder and badder and badder and badder and
badder and badder and badder and badder and badder
and badder and badder and badder and badder and
badder and badder and badder and badder and badder
and badder and badder and badder and badder and
badder and badder and badder and badder and badder
and badder and badder and badder and badder and
badder and badder and badder and badder and badder
and badder and badder and badder and badder and
badder and badder and badder and badder and badder
and badder and badder and badder and badder and
badder and badder and badder and badder and badder
and badder and badder and badder and badder and
badder and badder and badder and badder and badder
and badder and badder and badder and badder and
badder and badder and badder and badder and badder
and badder and badder and badder and badder and
badder and badder and badder and badder and badder
and badder and badder and badder and badder and
badder and badder and badder and badder and badder
and badder and badder and badder and badder and

badder and badder.

THE END

Very Bad Plane, Ship, and Bread Van Riddles

Q: Why did the plane crash?
A: Because the pilot was a loaf of bread.

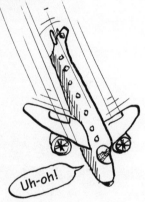

Q: Why did the ship crash?
A: Because the captain was a loaf of bread.

Q: Why did the bread van crash?

A: Accident investigators believe that it was due to a combination of factors, including high winds, icy roads, a dirty windshield, brake failure, four flat tires, and an indicator malfunction (plus the fact that the driver was a loaf of bread).

163

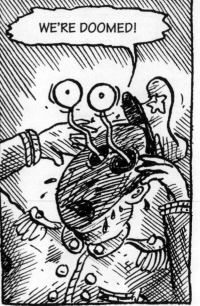

169

170

YES!